Goal Getter!

To all of the young kids who continue to inspire me by smiling, having fun and trying their best. And to Lucy, Oscar, and Olivia – I love to watch you play — AB

For Mama and the rest of my big, lovely families — JM

For Nanny Maz and Grandad, who nurtured my creativity and taught me to be brave enough to reach for my dreams — JG

HarperCollins*Children'sBooks*

HarperCollins*Publishers*
Australia • Brazil • Canada • France • Germany • Holland • India
Italy • Japan • Mexico • New Zealand • Poland • Spain • Sweden
Switzerland • United Kingdom • United States of America

HarperCollins acknowledges the Traditional Custodians of the land upon which we live and work, and pays respect to Elders past and present.

First published in Australia in 2022
by HarperCollins*Children'sBooks*
a division of HarperCollins*Publishers* Australia Pty Limited
Gadigal Country
Level 13, 201 Elizabeth Street, Sydney NSW 2000
ABN 36 009 913 517 harpercollins.com.au

A catalogue record for this book is available from the National Library of Australia

ISBN 978 1 4607 6279 0 (paperback)
ISBN 978 1 4607 1536 9 (ebook)

Cover design by Kristy Lund-White
Cover illustrations by Jade Goodwin
Ash Barty photograph by Nic Morley
Jade Goodwin photograph by Travis De Vries
Typeset in Bembo Infant MT by Kelli Lonergan
Printed and bound in Australia by McPherson's Printing Group

MIX
Paper from
responsible sources
FSC
www.fsc.org   FSC® C001695

ASH BARTY PRESENTS... Little ASH

Goal Getter!

BOOK 4

Written by
JASMIN McGAUGHEY

Illustrated by
JADE GOODWIN

HarperCollins*Children's Books*

Chapter One

Hi there! I'm Ash. I'm seven years old and I love to play sports.

Today, I'm playing touch footy, and my team's about to **win!**

The sun is hot. The grass on the oval is itchy. I'm thirsty. But none of these things matter right now because I have the ball, and I'm an **excellent** goal getter! I need to get the ball to the other end of the field so we can score a try.

I run past Jada, who's on the other team. She tries to tap my shoulder but she trips over! I dodge past Omari, the tallest kid in our class, and his fingers almost touch my arm, but they miss.

The kids watching on the sidelines **cheer** for me!

I'm about to throw a cut-out
pass to my best friend, James, who's
on the wing. That means the ball
has to fly to the other end of the
oval so James can catch it and
score the try. James is excellent

at **catching** things, which is one of the reasons he's my best friend. He's great at catching basketballs, cricket balls, and **popcorn** when I throw it to him on movie nights!

I push off on my right foot and move the ball to my side. Then I throw the ball as far as I can!

It spins in the air and everyone nearby dives for it. But nobody catches it. Not even James.

Oh no!

The ball lands in a puddle of mud and the bell for class rings at the exact same time!

'We lost!' James says, as I run over to him.

'How could this happen?' I ask. I cross my arms and try not to cry.

'It's all right, Ash! It's just a game. It's okay to lose sometimes.'

But it **doesn't** feel okay to lose! My throat feels tight. I walk to the ball. My feet feel heavy, they

drag across the grass. I pick up
the ball and we walk back to our
classroom.

'What if losing this game means
I've **lost** all my footy skills?' I ask
James.

'You haven't lost your skills, Ash,' James says. 'You're a great footy player.'

But I don't know if I believe him. I think I might have lost my footy talents.

I pull my hat down low on my head. Maybe I have lost **ALL** my sports talents.

Chapter Two

When Dad picks me up from
school, I jump into the back seat
next to my sister Sara. Ali is sitting
in the seat next to Dad. Usually,
Sara, Ali and I **race** to get the
front seat, but not today.

'Did something happen, Ash?'
Dad asks me.

'You look **sad**,' Sara tells me.

'I don't want to talk about it,'
I say.

'All right,' Dad says. 'Well, when
you're ready you can come and
talk to me. I know some things.'

'I know things too, Dad,' I tell
him.

'Of course you do, Ash.' He
looks in his mirror and gives me
a wink.

'Hey!' Sara says. 'When we get home, can we play elastics? The **winner** gets out of doing the dishes.'

'Yes! I'd love that,' Ali says.

I rest my head against the window. I don't say anything.

When we get home, I'm the first one to put my school bag and lunchbox away. I get changed and **run** outside before Sara and Ali ask me to play elastics with them.

I don't want to let them down. But I don't feel like playing elastics with Sara and Ali. I don't feel like playing any games.

I'm **afraid** I will lose again.

Chapter Three

I'm sitting in a tree in our
backyard. The tree is smooth and
very comfy. I **like** to sit and watch
the green ants walk in a line along
the trunk. I also **like** the smell
of the flowers. Mum and I water
the plants every Sunday morning.

It feels good to help look after the garden.

This is one of my **happy places**. It's also my thinking place.

I want to think of a way out of playing elastics with my sisters.

'Ash!' Sara appears below me.

'Ahh!' I wobble on the branch. 'You **scared** me!'

Sara giggles as Ali comes outside too.

'What are you doing in that tree, Ash?' Ali asks. 'Let's play elastics.'

'I don't want to play elastics,'
I say. I climb down the tree. Maybe
I can hide away in my room.

'Do you want to play a **board
game**?' Sara asks.

I think about losing a board
game. 'Nope,' I say.

'I know what you'll want to
play,' Ali says.

I stop before I get inside the
house. Ali's always good at
thinking of **games** for us to play.
Mum says she's really creative.

'What is it?' I ask her.

'Mini golf!' Ali says.

'Ohh,' I say. Mini golf is awesome. It's like the golf that adults play, but there are lots of **fun** things in the way of you getting the ball into the hole.

'Please, please, please!' Ali says.

'Please!' says Sara.

I take a big breath. I **really** don't want to play. But it's very hard to say no to my big sisters.

'Okay,' I say. 'Let's play mini golf.'

Chapter Four

My sisters and I set up a mini-golf

course in our backyard.

'Here, let's stick these together!'

Sara holds empty toilet rolls

and sticky tape. 'We can make

a **tunnel** for the golf ball to go

through.'

I help Sara sticky tape the toilet rolls, and we lay the tunnel down on the grass. We put a cup at the end of the tunnel.

We make cardboard boxes with holes cut out. We have a doll's house that the ball can roll

through, and we make a ramp with a cutting board from the kitchen. The whole course looks **amazing!**

'We're really good at this,' I say.

'You bet we are,' says Ali.

'Okay, Ash. Do you want to go **first**?' Sara hands me a golf club she got from the garage. It's heavy in my hands.

The first part of the course is the tunnel made of toilet rolls. I have to get the ball through the tunnel and into the cup at the end.

I wiggle my shoulders. I wiggle my hips. I hold the club tight and swing it just a little bit. I tap the ball with the club, and it goes into the toilet roll tunnel.

The ball shoots out of the tunnel and goes straight into the cup.

'Yay!' My hands fly into the sky. 'I got it! **A hole in one!**'

'Good job, Ash!' Ali says.

We keep playing. We're all really good at mini golf. We have so much fun. I **forget** all about losing lunchtime footy today.

Finally, it comes to the last shot. It's super tricky. I need to hit the ball up the cutting-board ramp. The ball has to go through the

teeny-tiny door of the doll's house,
and then it has to make it through
some weeds and into the big cup at
the end.

'Let's say whoever makes this
shot **wins** the whole entire game!'
Ali says.

'And the loser has to do the dishes tonight!' Sara adds with a smile.

Suddenly my tummy tightens.

'That's **not fair**,' I say.

'It's okay, Ash!' Ali says.

Sara takes the club from me. 'I'll go first.'

Sara hits the ball, and it moves fast! We watch it **fly** up the ramp and go straight into the doll's house. It stops in the weeds. Sara completes

one more shot and the ball goes into

the cup. Her score is two.

'Great, Sara,' Ali says and then

takes the club. 'My turn.'

Ali hits the ball at the right

angle, and it makes it all the way

to the cup, but it doesn't go in. She

taps it softly once more. Her score

is also two.

Now it's my turn.

I hold the club, swing it, and

hit the ball. But I hit the ball

too hard! It shoots up the ramp.
It flies high into the sky and over
our back fence!

I've lost a game for the second
time today and now I have to do
the dishes.

My eyes feel **scratchy**, as if I might cry.

'It's okay, Ash,' Sara says.

But I'm very sad. I don't think I will ever play sport **ever** again.

Chapter Five

The next day is Friday. I go to

school, but I **don't** play handball

in the morning before class.

I **don't** play tag at morning tea.

And I definitely **avoid** lunchtime

footy. I'm very lucky we don't

have any P.E. today.

'I'm sorry you're sad about the footy game yesterday,' James tells me at the end of school.

'I'll be okay,' I tell James. 'Tonight, is Friday night footy. Mum and Dad will buy pizza and

I'll get to watch the footy! Friday nights are the **best!**'

'I don't watch footy on Fridays,' James says. 'We go to my grandma's and watch her **favourite** shows!'

'Okay. Well, maybe I can see you tomorrow?' I ask.

'**Fantastic!**' James says, and we walk over to our families waiting for us outside the school gate.

I **miss out** on the front seat again. This time Sara is there, and

I sit next to Ali in the back. Dad
drives us home and then I help
Mum and Dad order pizzas. Pizza
is a **delicious**, amazing food. I like
to eat mine with lots of toppings,
including pineapple.

We set up our pizzas and soft drink on our brown coffee table and Dad turns the footy on.

The game is **exciting** from the start. Our team starts out strong and they score the first try. But the other team catches up and soon they're winning. I'm on the edge of my seat the whole time. Dad and Mum cheer for their favourite players. I join in. My favourite player is the **smart** halfback.

Soon it's the last few minutes of the game, and our team has to score a try to win.

I **stand up** because I have way too much energy to sit down.

'Come on!' Dad shouts with a smile.

'You've got this!' Mum says.

Ali and Sara are sitting on their knees on the carpet gripping each other's hands.

My legs are shaky with nervous energy.

The halfback gets the ball and throws it toward the winger. The ball flies smoothly in the air and passes three players. The winger reaches their hands out to catch the ball, but it slips right **through** their fingers and out of bounds!

Two seconds later the siren sounds loudly, and the referee blows their whistle. The game has ended.

I **fall** to my knees and tug at my hair. 'They lost!' I cry.

Our favourite team **lost** its first game of the season. It feels exactly like losing the lunchtime footy game yesterday. My heart feels like it has **broken** into a million tiny pieces.

I look at Dad. I'm worried he'll be even more upset than me. Dad

is shaking his head while he holds
a slice of pizza, but he doesn't look
that sad.

'Dad! Didn't you see that they
lost?' I ask. 'Aren't you **upset**?'

Dad gives me a long look.
'Come sit up here, Ash.'

I sit on our big comfy blue
couch next to him and he turns
to face me.

'Now,' Dad says. He puts his
slice of pizza down on his plate. 'It's
perfectly okay to lose a game every

once in a while,' he says. 'We don't always have to win.'

'I **like** winning, though, and I definitely don't like losing.'

Dad laughs. 'I know. I don't like losing either, but we can't win all the time. Plus, we can learn something **special** from losing.'

'Like what?' I ask.

'To pick ourselves up, be proud we did our best, and try again next time,' he says.

'So I shouldn't get upset when I lose?' I ask.

'It's all right to be upset,' Dad says. 'But you have to try not to let the feeling **take you over**. Do you understand?'

'I think so,' I say.

He pats my back and gives me his own slice of pizza.

Chapter Six

I wake up the next morning and
I feel **jittery**. My body wants to
move! My legs want to run. My
arms want to swing a racquet. I've
missed playing footy and tennis
at school. I've also missed playing
elastics with my sisters.

'Do you want to go to the tennis courts today, Ash?' Dad asks me. 'We can pick James up on the way.'

'Yes please, Dad! I've **missed** playing sport.'

'It's only been two days,' Dad says.

'That's **ages!**'

I get ready quickly and we pick James up from his house.

'Hey, Ash. What are we doing today?' he asks me.

'We're going to play some tennis.'

'Yay!' says James.

At the tennis centre, Dad grabs a cold drink while James and I run onto the court. Because James doesn't play tennis all the time, like me, he doesn't own a racquet and he has to borrow one of mine.

James and I **warm up** first.

I teach him how to do all the

different kinds of strokes.

'This is hard,' he says.

'You've got this!' I tell him.

James and I play a **mini tennis**

match next. He serves the ball just like I show him, and I hit it back to him. It's great. But I'm so tired from watching footy last night that I'm slow. I'm so **slow** that I miss the ball more than once!

James wins the first set!

I feel my tummy tighten and my eyes get itchy. But I take a **deep breath**.

'Good job, James!' I tell him.

James gives me a thumbs up and jumps up and down. We keep playing and James doesn't mind when I win a set, and I don't mind when James wins another set. He even wins the whole match!

I feel happy, because even though I didn't win, I still had **fun!**

When it gets too hot Dad calls us over.

'Let's go and get you two some ice blocks,' he says.

'Yes please!' James and I say at the same time. We look at each other and crack up laughing.

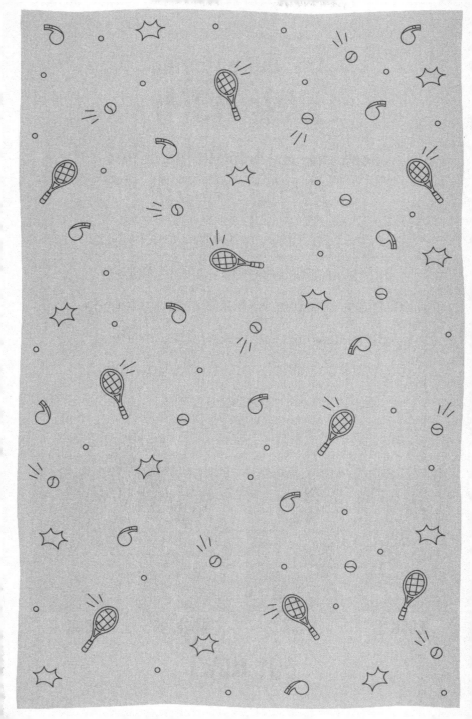

Are you enjoying Little ASH?

Read the first book in the series, Perfect Match!

Ash loves to play sport. She's tried karate, softball, netball and gymnastics. But none of those sports give her that tingly feeling, the one where you know it's something you'll absolutely love to do. How will Ash ever choose?

BOOK 1

BOOK 2

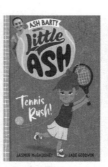

BOOK 3

BOOK 4

OUT NOW!